My Humpty Dumpty
Book of Nursery Rhymes

Brown Watson

ENGLAND

HEY DIDDLE, DIDDLE

Hey diddle, diddle,
The cat and the fiddle,
The cow jumped over the moon.

2

The little dog laughed
To see such sport,
And the dish ran away with the spoon.

WEE WILLIE WINKIE

Wee Willie Winkie
Runs through the town,
Upstairs and downstairs
In his nightgown.

4

Rapping at the window,
Crying through the lock,
Are the children all in bed,
For it's past eight o'clock.

5

MARY, MARY

Mary, Mary, quite contrary,
How does your garden grow?
With silver bells and cockle shells
And pretty maids all in a row.

SEE-SAW MARGERY DAW

See-saw Margery Daw,
Johnny shall have a new master;
He shall have but a penny a day,
Because he can't work any faster.

7

ONE, TWO, BUCKLE MY SHOE

One, two, buckle my shoe;
Three, four, knock at the door;
Five, six, pick up sticks;
Seven, eight, lay them straight;

8

Nine, ten, my fat hen;

Eleven, twelve,
dig and delve.

9

SING A SONG OF SIXPENCE

Sing a song of sixpence,
A pocket full of rye;
Four and twenty blackbirds
Baked in a pie.

10

When the pie was opened,
The birds began to sing;
Wasn't that a dainty dish
To set before the King.

11

The King was in his counting house
Counting out his money;
The Queen was in the parlour
Eating bread and honey.

12

The maid was in the garden
Hanging out the clothes;
When down came a blackbird
And pecked off her nose.

13

DOCTOR FOSTER

Doctor Foster went to Gloucester
In a shower of rain;
He stepped in a puddle,
Right up to his middle,
And never went there again.

EENSY, WEENSY SPIDER

Eensy, weensy spider,
Climbed the water spout.
Down came the rain
And washed the spider out.

15

HOT CROSS BUNS

Hot cross buns!
Hot cross buns!
One a penny,
Two a penny,
Hot cross buns!

If you have no daughters,
Give them to your sons.
One a penny,
Two a penny,
Hot cross buns!

LITTLE BO-PEEP

Little Bo-Peep has lost her sheep,
And doesn't know where to find them

18

Leave them alone,
And they'll come home,
Wagging their tails behind them.

ROCK-A-BYE BABY

Rock-a-bye baby,
On the tree top,
When the wind blows
The cradle will rock.

20

When the bough breaks,
The cradle will fall –
Down will come baby,
Cradle and all!

21

THIS LITTLE PIGGY

This little piggy went to market,
This little piggy stayed at home,
This little piggy had roast beef,
This little piggy had none,
And this little piggy cried,
"Wee, wee, wee," all the way home!

TO BED, TO BED

"To bed, to bed!" said Sleepy Head.
"Tarry a while," said Slow.
"Put on the pan," said Greedy Ann.
"We'll sup before we go."

23

MARY HAD A LITTLE LAMB

Mary had a little lamb,
Its fleece was white as snow,
And everywhere that Mary went
That lamb was sure to go.

24

It followed her to school one day,
That was against the rule;
It made the children laugh and play,
To see a lamb at school.

25

JACK SPRAT

Jack Sprat could eat no fat,
His wife could eat no lean,
And so between them both,
They licked the platter clean.

26

Jack ate all the lean,
Joan ate all the fat,
The bone they picked it clean,
Then gave it to the cat.

LITTLE POLLY FLINDERS

Little Polly Flinders
Sat among the cinders,
Warming her pretty little toes;

Her mother came and caught her,
And whipped her little daughter
For spoiling her nice new clothes.

PAT-A-CAKE

Pat-a-cake, pat-a-cake, baker's man,
Bake me a cake as fast as you can;
Pat it and prick it and mark it with B,
And put it in the oven for baby and me

TOMMY TUCKER

Little Tommy Tucker
Sang for his supper;
What shall we give him?
White bread and butter.
How shall he cut it without any knife?
How will he marry, without any wife?

31

LITTLE BOY BLUE

Little Boy Blue,
Come blow your horn,
The sheep's in the meadow,
The cow's in the corn.

Where is the boy
Who looks after the sheep?
He's under the haystack,
Fast asleep!

33

HALF A POUND OF TUPPENNY RICE

Half a pound of tuppenny rice,
Half a pound of treacle,
That's the way the money goes,
Pop goes the weasel!

Up and down the city road,
In and out the Eagle,
That's the way the money goes,
Pop goes the weasel!

THERE WAS A CROOKED MAN

There was a crooked man,
And he walked a crooked mile,
He found a crooked sixpence
Against a crooked stile;

He bought a crooked cat,
Which caught a crooked mouse,
And they all lived together
In a little crooked house.

TOM THE PIPER'S SON

Tom, Tom, the piper's son,
Stole a pig and away did run;
The pig was eat and Tom was beat,
And Tom went howling down the street

COBBLER, COBBLER

Cobbler, cobbler, mend my shoe,
Get it done by half-past-two;
Stitch it up and stitch it down,
Then I'll give you half-a-crown.

LADYBIRD, LADYBIRD

Ladybird, ladybird,
Fly away home.
Your house is on fire,
Your children are gone;

40

All except one,
And that's little Ann,
And she crept under
The warming pan.

HUMPTY DUMPTY

Humpty Dumpty sat on a wall,
Humpty Dumpty had a great fall.

All the King's horses
And all the King's men,
Couldn't put Humpty together again.

43

ROUND AND ROUND THE GARDEN

Round and round the garden
Like a teddy bear.
One step, two steps,
Tickle me under there.

Round and round the haystack
Went the little mouse.
One step, two steps,
In his little house.

45

RING-A-RING O'ROSES

Ring-a-ring o'roses,
A pocket full of posies,
A-tishoo! A-tishoo!
We all fall down.

TWINKLE, TWINKLE, LITTLE STAR

Twinkle, twinkle, little star,
How I wonder what you are!
Up above the world so high,
Like a diamond in the sky.

47

DING, DONG, BELL

Ding, dong, bell,
Pussy's in the well.
Who put her in?
Little Johnny Thin.

Who pulled her out?
Little Tommy Stout.
What a naughty boy was that
To try to drown poor pussycat,
Who never did him any harm,
But killed all the mice
In his father's barn.

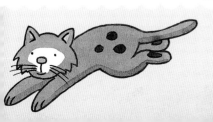

GOOSEY GANDER

Goosey, goosey gander,
Where shall I wander?
Upstairs and downstairs,
In my lady's chamber.

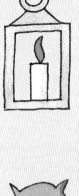

Where I met an old man,
Who wouldn't say his prayers,
I took him by the left leg,
And threw him down the stairs.

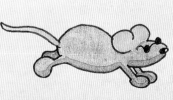

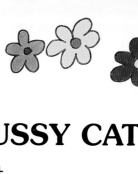

PUSSY CAT, PUSSY CAT

Pussy cat, pussy cat,
Where have you been?
I've been up to London,
To visit the Queen.

Pussy cat, pussy cat,
What did you there?
I frightened a little mouse,
Under a chair.

LITTLE JACK HORNER

Little Jack Horner sat in a corner,
Eating his Christmas pie;
He put in his thumb,
And pulled out a plum,
And said "What a good boy am I!"

54

COCK-A-DOODLE DOO!

Cock-a-doodle doo!
My dame has lost her shoe,
My master's lost his fiddling stick,
And knows not what to do.

BAA, BAA, BLACK SHEEP

Baa, baa, black sheep,
Have you any wool?
Yes, sir, yes, sir,
Three bags full.

56

One for the master,
And one for the dame,
And one for the little boy
Who lives down the lane.

I'M A LITTLE TEAPOT

I'm a little teapot,
Short and stout,
Here's my handle,
Here's my spout.

When I see the teacups,
Hear me shout:
Tip me up and pour me out!

59

THE QUEEN OF HEARTS

The Queen of Hearts
She made some tarts,
All on a summer's day;
The Knave of Hearts
He stole the tarts,
And took them right away.

The King of Hearts
Called for the tarts,
And beat the Knave full sore;
The Knave of Hearts
Brought back the tarts,
And vowed he'd steal no more.

61

RAIN, RAIN, GO AWAY

Rain, rain, go away,
Come back another day,
All the children want to play.
Rain, rain, go to Spain,
Never show your face again.

IT'S RAINING,
IT'S POURING

It's raining, it's pouring,
The old man is snoring.
He went to bed
And bumped his head,
And couldn't get up in the morning!

CURLY LOCKS

Curly Locks, Curly Locks,
Will you be mine?
You shall not wash dishes,
Nor yet feed the swine;

64

You'll sit on a cushion
And sew a fine seam,
And feed upon strawberries,
Sugar and cream.

POLLY PUT THE KETTLE ON

Polly put the kettle on,
Polly put the kettle on,
Polly put the kettle on,
We'll all have tea.

Sukey take it off again,
Sukey take it off again,
Sukey take it off again,
They've all gone away.

OLD KING COLE

Old King Cole was a merry old soul,
And a merry old soul was he;

68

He called for his pipe,
And he called for his bowl,
And he called for his fiddlers three.

69

LITTLE MISS MUFFET

Little Miss Muffet
Sat on her tuffet,
Eating her curds and whey;
There came a big spider,
Who sat down beside her,
And frightened Miss Muffet away.

JACK AND JILL

Jack and Jill went up the hill,
To fetch a pail of water;
Jack fell down and broke his crown,
And Jill came tumbling after.

RUB-A-DUB-DUB

Rub-a-dub-dub,
Three men in a tub,
And who do you think they be?

72

The butcher, the baker,
The candlestick-maker,
And up they jump all three!

73

THREE BLIND MICE

Three blind mice, three blind mice,
See how they run, see how they run!
They all ran after the farmer's wife,

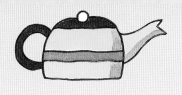

Who cut off their tails
With the carving knife,
Did you ever see
Such a thing in your life,
As three blind mice?

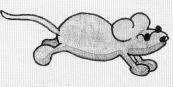

TWO LITTLE DICKIE BIRDS

Two little dickie birds sitting on a wall
One named Peter,
One named Paul.

Fly away, Peter!
Fly away, Paul!
Come back, Peter!
Come back, Paul!

77

JACK BE NIMBLE

Jack be nimble,
Jack be quick,
Jack jump over
The candlestick.

HIGGELDY, PIGGELDY

Higgeldy, piggeldy, my black hen,
She lays eggs for gentlemen;
Sometimes nine and sometimes ten,
Higgeldy, piggeldy, my black hen.

SIMPLE SIMON

Simple Simon met a pieman
Going to the fair;
Said Simple Simon to the pieman:
"Let me taste your ware."

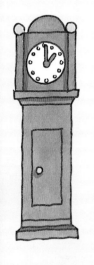

Said the pieman to Simple Simon:
"Show me first your penny."
Said Simple Simon to the pieman:
"Indeed, I have not any."

OLD MOTHER HUBBARD

Old Mother Hubbard
Went to the cupboard,
To get her poor doggy a bone;

But when she got there,
The cupboard was bare,
And so the poor doggy had none!

THE GRAND OLD DUKE OF YORK

Oh, the grand old Duke of York,
He had ten thousand men;

84

He marched them up to the top of the hill,
And he marched them down again.
And when they were up, they were up,
And when they were down, they were down,
And when they were only halfway up,
They were neither up nor down.

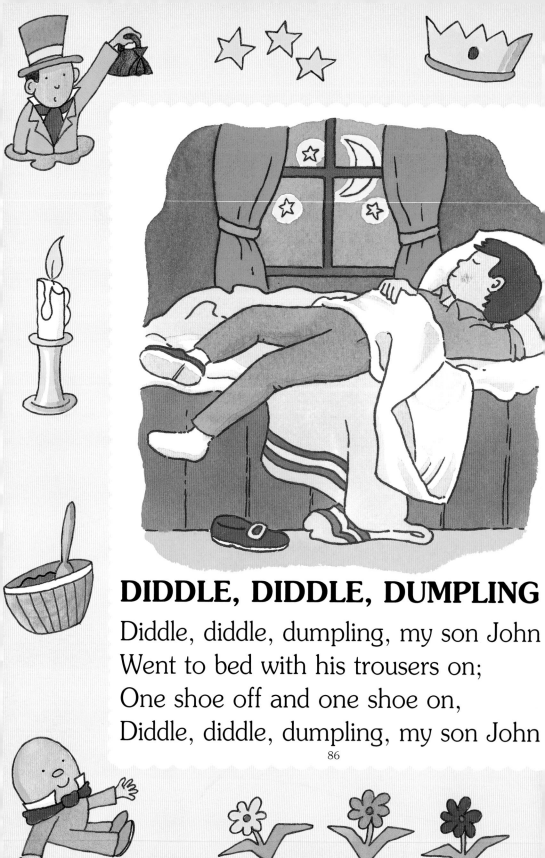

DIDDLE, DIDDLE, DUMPLING

Diddle, diddle, dumpling, my son John
Went to bed with his trousers on;
One shoe off and one shoe on,
Diddle, diddle, dumpling, my son John

HICKORY, DICKORY DOCK

Hickory, dickory dock,
The mouse ran up the clock.
The clock struck one,
The mouse ran down,
Hickory, dickory dock.

87

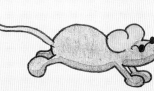

TO MARKET, TO MARKET

To market, to market,
To buy a fat pig,
Home again, home again,
Jiggety jig.

To market, to market,
To buy a fat hog,
Home again, home again,
Jiggety jog.

89

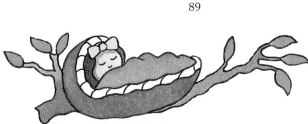

THERE WAS AN OLD WOMAN

There was an old woman,
Who lived in a shoe,
She had so many children
She didn't know what to do;

90

She gave them some broth,
Without any bread,
She whipped them all soundly,
And sent them to bed.

I HAD A LITTLE NUT TREE

I had a little nut tree,
Nothing would it bear
But a silver nutmeg
And a golden pear.

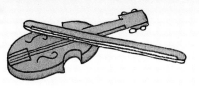

The King of Spain's daughter
Came to visit me,
And all for the sake
Of my little nut tree.

93

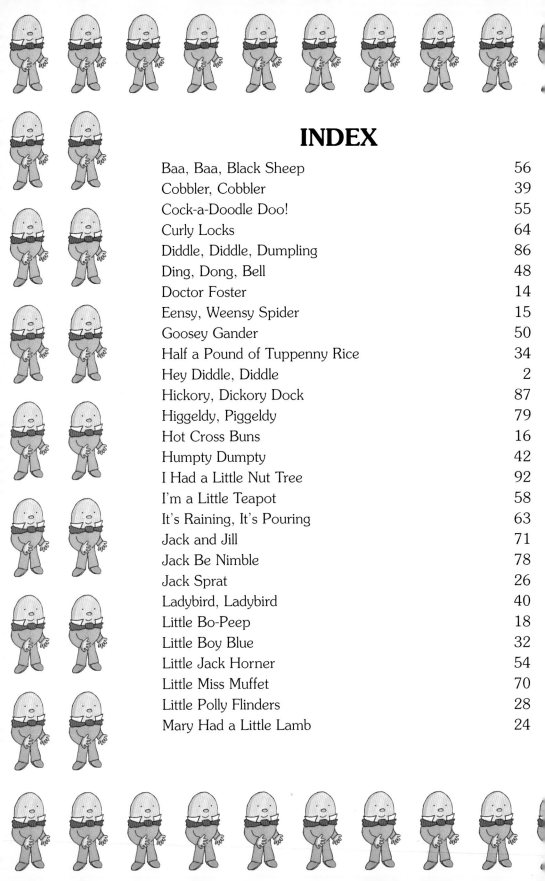

INDEX

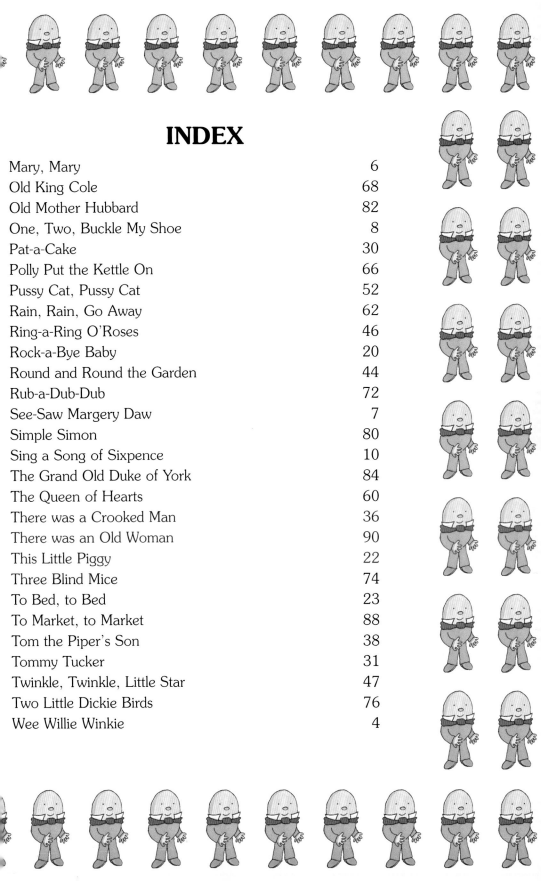

INDEX

This edition first published 2001 by
Brown Watson, The Old Mill,
76 Fleckney Road, Kibworth Beauchamp,
Leicestershire LE8 0HG

ISBN: 978-0-7097-1440-8

Reprinted 2002, 2003, 2004 (twice), 2005 (twice), 2006, 2008, 2009, 2011

Printed in China